All children have
a great ambition to read
to themselves . . .

and a sense of achievement when they can do so.
The **read it yourself** *series has been devised to*
satisfy their ambition. Since many children learn
from the Ladybird Key Words Reading Scheme,
these stories have been based to a large extent
on the Key Words List, and the tales chosen are
those with which children are likely to be familiar.

The series can of course be used as
supplementary reading for any reading scheme.
Jack and the Beanstalk is intended for children
reading up to Book 4c of the Ladybird Reading
Scheme. The following words are additional to
the vocabulary used at that level –

Jack, money, food, but, throws, beanstalk,
giant, wife, fee, fi, fo, fum, cupboard, bag,
sleep, runs, stole, again, after, hen, harp,
axe, killed, magic, beans, now, garden

A list of other titles at the same level will be
found on the back cover.

Jack and the Beanstalk

by Fran Hunia
illustrated by Brian Price Thomas

Ladybird Books Loughborough

Jack and his Mummy have no money
and no food in the house.

All they have is one cow.

She is a good cow,
and she gives good milk,
but Jack and his Mummy want food.

"We have to get some food,"

says Jack's Mummy.

"Off you go with the cow, Jack.

Go and get some money for the cow,

and then we can get

some things for tea."

"I will see what I can do,"

says Jack.

Away he goes with the cow.

He sees a man.

"What a good cow you have,"

says the man.

"Yes," says Jack. "She is a good cow,

and she gives good milk,

but we can not keep her.

We have to get some money

for food."

"I have no money," says the man,

"but I have some magic beans.

Please give me the cow,

and you can have my magic beans."

"That will be good," says Jack.

"Here you are. You have the cow,

and I will have the magic beans."

Jack thanks the man

and then he goes home.

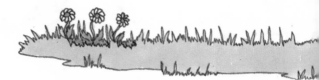

Jack gives the magic beans
to his Mummy.
"Look," he says. "We can have
beans for tea."

His Mummy looks at the beans.
"Is that all you have?" she says.
"I do not want beans."

She throws the beans away,
into the garden,
and Jack has to go to bed
with no tea.

The magic beans come up.

They make a big, big beanstalk.

"What a big beanstalk," says Jack.

"It makes the house and the trees

look little. I will go

and see what is up there."

"No," says Jack's Mummy.

"Keep away, Jack.

There will be danger up there."

"Yes," says Jack. "There will be
danger, but I have to go and see
what is up there."

His Mummy lets him go.

Jack goes up and up and up.

He sees a big house.

It is a giant's house,
but Jack wants to go in.

"No, stop," says the giant's wife.
"You can not come in here."

"Please let me come in," says Jack.
"I will be good."

The giant's wife likes children.

She lets Jack come in,

and she gives him some food

and some milk.

Jack thanks her.

The giant comes home.

He says, " Fee, fi, fo, fum,

little children, here I come."

The giant's wife puts Jack

in the cupboard.

She says to the giant,

" There are no children here,

but I have some food for you."

The giant has his tea

and then he says,

" Get me my money bag."

The giant's wife gets him

the money bag,

and then she goes off to bed.

Jack looks at the money bag.

"The giant stole that money bag

from my Daddy," he says.

"I have to get it."

The giant goes to sleep
and Jack gets the money bag.

He runs away down the beanstalk
with it. The giant sleeps on.

Jack gives the money bag
to his Mummy.
"Was this Daddy's money bag?"
he says.

"Yes, it was," says his Mummy.
"The giant stole it."

Jack goes

up the beanstalk again.

He comes

to the giant's house,

and he sees

the giant's wife.

" I do not want you

to come in,"

says the giant's wife.

" The giant

will come home,

and he will be after you."

" Please let me in," says Jack.

The giant's wife likes Jack.
She lets him in and gives him
some food and milk.

Then the giant comes home.
He says, " Fee, fi, fo, fum,
little children, here I come."

Jack gets into the cupboard.

"There are no children here,"

says the giant's wife,

"but I have some food for you."

The giant has his tea,

and then he says,

"Get me my magic hen."

The giant's wife gives him

the magic hen,

and then she goes off to bed.

Jack sees the magic hen.

"The giant stole that hen from my
Daddy," he says. "I have to get it."

The giant goes to sleep,
then Jack gets the hen
and runs away with it.

The giant sleeps on.

Jack goes down the beanstalk.

He gives the hen to his Mummy.

" Look, Mummy," he says.
" Can we keep this hen?"

"Yes," says his Mummy. "The giant
stole that hen from Daddy."

Jack goes up the beanstalk again.

He goes to the giant's house.

"Please go away,"

says the giant's wife.

"You can not come in here.

The giant will get you."

"Please let me come in," says Jack.

The giant's wife wants to help Jack.

She lets him come in,

and she gives him

some food and milk.

The giant comes home.

He says, " Fee, fi, fo, fum,

little children, here I come."

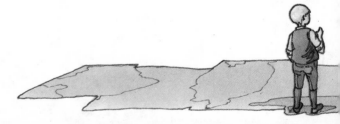

41

"There are no children here,"

says the giant's wife,

"but I have some food for you."

She gives the giant his tea.

Then the giant says,

"Get me my magic harp."

The giant's wife gives him

the magic harp,

and then she goes

off to bed.

43

The magic harp plays for the giant,

and he goes to sleep.

Jack looks at the harp.

"That was my Daddy's harp,"

he says. "I will get it."

Jack gets the magic harp,

and runs off with it,

but the harp says, "Help, help!"

The giant gets up

and runs after Jack.

Jack runs to the beanstalk,

and the giant keeps on after him.

Down goes Jack,

and down goes the giant.

Down, and down, and down.

Jack sees his home.

He says, "Mummy, Mummy,
get the axe.
The giant is after me."

Jack's Mummy runs to get the axe.
She gives it to him.

Down comes the beanstalk
and the giant is killed.

"That is good," says Jack's Mummy.
"The giant is no danger to us now.
Let us go and get
some good things for tea."